DISNEY

PRINCESS

My Princess Collection

Belle

Who Could Love a Beast?

Book Four

Chapter One

I'm Princess Belle. I live with the Prince in a castle that people used to say was haunted. In a way, they were right. Once upon a time, a terrible beast lived here.

Before I became a princess, I lived with my father, an inventor. Our neighbors didn't understand us. They wondered why my father spent all day creating strange inventions and why I loved reading books so much.

Gaston was one of our neighbors. He was a hunter and thought himself a prize catch. I thought he was very rude. He often called me the "luckiest girl in town" because he had decided to marry me without asking me how I felt. I couldn't stand him!

Chapter Two

One day after Papa left home to enter his latest invention in a competition, Gaston stopped by.

"Say you'll marry me!" he said.

"I don't deserve you," I said sarcastically as I pushed him out the door. I couldn't believe Gaston thought I would marry him just because he was good-looking! The man I planned to marry had to be beautiful on the *inside*.

Later that evening, our horse, Phillipe, returned home without Papa. Something must have gone wrong! I climbed onto Phillipe's back, and he took me to find Papa.

We finally arrived at a huge castle. It looked empty. The door was open.

I crept quietly through the castle, looking for Papa. I was afraid of what might live in such a cold, forbidding place. But I was more afraid for Papa's safety, so I continued searching for him.

I finally found Papa locked in the dungeon! He was ill. "Who did this to you?" I cried.

"What are you doing?" a voice growled behind me. It was a beast! He had giant, sharp teeth and horns on his head.

"I've come for my father," I said. "He's sick."

"There's nothing you can do. He's my prisoner," the Beast replied.

"Take me instead," I said.

The Beast looked at me and cried out, "Done!"

Papa told the Beast to let me go, but the Beast ignored him and dragged him out of the castle.

Chapter Three

I didn't even get to say good-bye.

When the Beast returned, he showed me to my room. "You can go anywhere in the castle, but the West Wing is forbidden!" he growled before he left.

I was afraid, but I was more worried about Papa. I hoped he would make it home safely.

Suddenly, I heard voices. Looking around, I found a teapot named Mrs. Potts, and her son, a teacup named Chip. They were welcoming me to the castle. Was I dreaming?

Nearly every object in the house could talk!

A candelabrum named Lumiere opened the kitchen door for me, and the stove was stirring its own pot.

Everyone made me feel so comfortable that I was no longer afraid. But I did want to know what sort of magic made cups talk. And who or what was the Beast who lived here?

The answer was in the West Wing . . . I was sure of it!

Chapter Four

After dinner, I secretly crept into the West Wing. I found a room full of broken furniture and a painting of a handsome man who looked somewhat familiar.

Then I noticed a strange glow by the window. It was a red rose floating under a glass jar! Could this have something to do with—?

"Why did you come here?" bellowed the Beast, who had come up behind me.

He pulled the rose jar away and snarled. I didn't know why he was so angry. All I knew was that I had to leave the castle as soon as possible.

I hurried out of the castle to find Phillipe, who was waiting outside. But as we galloped through the woods, a pack of wolves surrounded us!

Suddenly, the Beast appeared. He bravely fought the wolves. He risked his life for me,

and he was badly hurt. I thought of riding away, but I knew I'd never forgive myself for leaving like that— no matter how horrible he was.

I struggled to pull the Beast onto Phillipe, and we returned to the castle.

Back at the castle, I cleaned the Beast's wounds.

"That hurts!" he yelped. "This happened because you ran away!"

"You should learn to control your temper," I snapped back.

He grunted but didn't say anything. I was beginning to think that the Beast had a bad temper, but a good heart.

"By the way, thank you . . . for saving my life," I said.

"You're welcome," he replied in a quiet voice.

Chapter Five

From then on, the Beast treated me very differently. On the outside he was still a monster, but on the inside he was a gentleman.

Over time, we became very good friends. We ate our meals together. He opened up his library to me, and he showed me his gardens. But he never explained about the glowing rose—or who he was, either.

One night, the Beast invited me to a special dinner. I wore a beautiful gold gown. When I entered the dining room, the Beast was waiting for me. Everything was perfect.

After dinner, we danced. Everyone watched from the doorway. They could tell that we were falling in love.

Later, I told the Beast I missed Papa. The Beast handed me a magic mirror that could show me whomever I wished to see. When I asked to see Papa, I saw that he was lying in the snow in the middle of the forest! He was very sick. I had to go help him right away.

"Take the mirror to remember me," the Beast said. He knew that I might never come back.

I hurried to the forest with Phillipe and found Papa. We headed home.

After I had left, the Beast noticed that the rose had lost some of its petals.

Once we got home, I put Papa to bed.
"How did you escape?" he cried.

"Papa," I said, "the Beast let me go."

Suddenly, Gaston and some of the villagers
were at our door. Gaston told the crowd that
Papa was crazy and had been talking about a
hideous beast. The villagers had come to take
Papa away—unless I agreed to marry Gaston.

"My father's not
craze! I can prove
it!" I said, pulling
out the magic
mirror. I asked
the mirror to
show me the
Beast. Everyone
gasped as the
Beast's image
appeared.

Gaston snatched the mirror from me. "The Beast will come after your children!" he cried to the villagers. "Let's kill the Beast!"

"He's not the monster!" I shouted. "*You* are!" But the villagers ignored me. They followed Gaston to the Beast's castle.

Chapter Six

When I arrived, Gaston and the Beast were already fighting on the castle roof. Gaston hurt the Beast! But then, Gaston lost his balance and fell to the ground.

"At least I saw you one last time," the Beast said to me. He was dying.

"I love you!" I said.

At that, a bright light surrounded the Beast's body and lifted him into the air.

When the light faded, the Beast had become . . . a prince. The very same prince from the painting I had seen in the West Wing.

Later, I found out that an Enchantress had cursed the young prince and turned him into the Beast because he had been selfish. She had also left the rose. If the last petal had fallen, the Beast would have remained a monster forever. But since he had learned to love and found someone to love him in return before the last petal fell—the spell had been broken!

Although, honestly, it didn't matter to me. The Beast . . . the Prince—I loved them both!